"HELLO READING books are a perfect introduction to reading. Brief sentences full of word repetition and full-color pictures stress visual clues to help a child take the first important steps toward reading. Mastering these story books will build children's reading confidence and give them the enthusiasm to stand on their own in the world of words."

—Bee Cullinan
Past President of the International Reading
Association, Professor in New York University's
Early Childhood and Elementary Education Program

"Readers aren't born, they're made. Desire is planted—planted by parents who work at it."

—Jim Trelease
author of *The Read Aloud Handbook*

"When I was a classroom reading teacher, I recognized the importance of good stories in making children understand that reading is more than just recognizing words. I saw that children who have ready access to story books get excited about reading. They also make noticeably greater gains in reading comprehension. The development of the HELLO READING stories grows out of this experience."

—Harriet Ziefert
M.A.T., New York University School of Education
Author, Language Arts Module,
Scholastic Early Childhood Program

For Carol Nicklaus

PUFFIN BOOKS
Viking Penguin Inc., 40 West 23rd Street,
New York, New York 10010, U.S.A.
Penguin Books Ltd., Harmondsworth, Middlesex, England
Penguin Books Australia Ltd., Ringwood, Victoria, Australia
Penguin Books Canada Limited, 2801 John St., Markham, Ontario, Canada
Penguin Books (N.Z.) Ltd., 182–190 Wairau Rd., Auckland 10, New Zealand

First published in 1987
3 5 7 9 10 8 6 4
Text copyright © Harriet Ziefert, 1987
Illustrations copyright © Richard Brown, 1987
All rights reserved

ISBN 0-14-050742-6 Library of Congress Catalog Card No: 86-82755
Printed in Singapore for Harriet Ziefert, Inc.

Nicky Upstairs and Down

Harriet Ziefert
Pictures by Richard Brown

PUFFIN BOOKS

Nicky lived with his mother
in a small house.

Nicky's house
had a downstairs...

and an upstairs.

When Nicky was playing,
his mother called,
"Nicky, where are you?
Are you upstairs?"

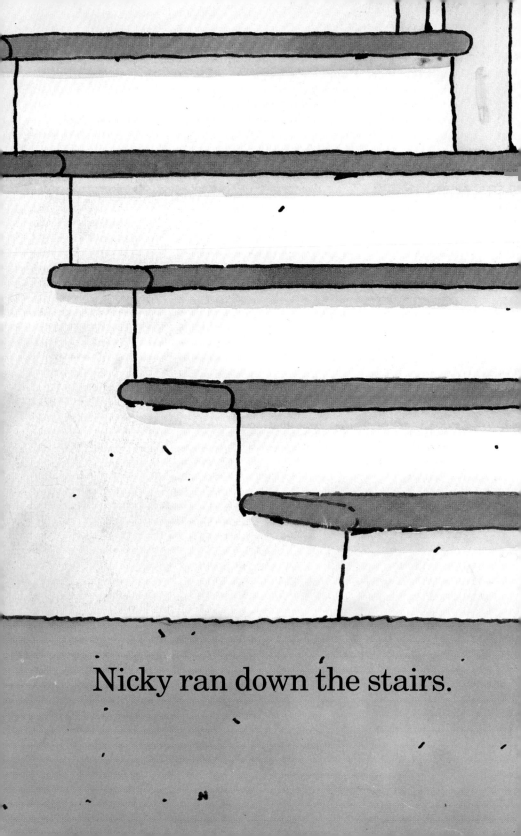

Nicky ran down the stairs.

He said, "Here I am!
I was up.
But now I'm down."

When Nicky was downstairs,
his mother called,
"Nicky, where are you?
Are you downstairs?"

Nicky ran up the stairs.

He said, "Here I am!
I was down.
But now I'm up."

Up and down.
Down and up.

Up and down the stairs —
all day long!

One day Nicky's mother called,
"Nicky, are you downstairs?"

No answer
from Nicky!

Then she called,
"Nicky, are you upstairs?"

No answer from Nicky.
No answer at all!

Nicky was hiding.
He was tired of running
up and down, down and up,
all day long!

His mother looked everywhere.
Upstairs...

and downstairs.

"Nicky," she said.
"Please come out.
Please!"

Nicky came out.
He ran halfway
up the stairs.

"Mama!" he called.
"Guess where I am?
I'm not upstairs.
I'm not downstairs."

"I'm right in the middle!"